SILVER
THE WILD TERROR

BY ADAM BLADE

ORCHARD

THE
ETERNAL
FLAME

THE SNOWY NORTH

THE SEA OF SERAPH

FISHING
VILLAGE

THE RAGING RIVER

THE WARLOCK'S STAFF

SilveR
THE WILD TERROR

With special thanks to
Allan Frewin Jones

To Henry

www.beastquest.co.uk

ORCHARD BOOKS
338 Euston Road, London NW1 3BH
Orchard Books Australia
Level 17/207 Kent St, Sydney, NSW 2000

A Paperback Original
First published in Great Britain in 2011

Beast Quest is a registered trademark of Beast Quest Limited
Series created by Beast Quest Limited, London

Text © Beast Quest Limited 2011
Inside illustrations by Pulsar Estudio (Beehive Illustration)
Cover illustration by Steve Sims © Orchard Books 2011

A CIP catalogue record for this book is available from
the British Library.

ISBN 978 1 40831 319 0

3 5 7 9 10 8 6 4 2

Printed and bound by CPI Group (UK) Ltd, Croydon, CR0 4YY

The paper and board used in this paperback are natural recyclable
products made from wood grown in sustainable forests. The
manufacturing processes conform to the environmental regulations of
the country of origin.

Orchard Books is a division of Hachette Children's Books,
an Hachette UK company

www.hachette.co.uk

Seraph

REDWELL

THE
EASTERN
FOREST

*T*om and Elenna are such fools! They thought their Quests were over and that my master was defeated. They were wrong! For now Malvel has the Warlock's Staff, hewn from the Tree of Being, and all kingdoms will soon be at his mercy.

We travel the land of Seraph, to find the Eternal Flame. And when we burn the Staff in the flame, our evil magic will be unstoppable. Tom and Elenna can chase us if they wish, but they'll find more than just Beasts lying in wait. They're alone this time, with no wizard to help them.

I hope Tom and Elenna are ready to meet me again. I've been waiting a long time for my revenge.

Yours, with glee, Petra the Witch

PROLOGUE

Two figures stood at the mouth of a dark cave. Icicles hung from the rocks around them and there was deep snow underfoot.

Evil Wizard Malvel, and Petra, gazed northwards, where a plume of bright flame flickered on a mountain top.

"Do you see it?" he hissed. "The Eternal Flame is where we will burn the Warlock's Staff and gain victory!"

"So why have we come to this cave?" Petra asked.

"Don't ask questions," snarled Malvel. "Just obey me!" He snapped his fingers and gestured into the cave.

Petra nodded and went scuttling into the gloom. Malvel folded his arms, a cruel smile twisting his lips as he listened to the whining and yapping of a dog.

A few moments later, Petra came out into the light, dragging a collie behind her at the end of a rope. The animal dug his paws into the packed dirt of the cave floor, but Petra had no trouble pulling him to the wizard's side.

"I have powerful new magic to work on this creature," Malvel said, looking disdainfully at the cowering dog.

The dog looked up at the wizard, pulling desperately on his lead, his eyes full of fear.

Malvel slid his hand into a pocket
and drew out a rosewood wand. It
had animal teeth embedded into it,
and scraps of fur hung from leather
thongs tied to the handle.

Petra wrinkled her nose. The
wand smelt disgusting!

Malvel glared at her. "Keep the
animal under control!" he growled.

The dog was fighting to get loose,
but Petra clung on to the rope and
kept him at the wizard's side. Malvel
aimed the point of the wand at the
dog's head. Immediately, the dog
sat down in the snow at the cave
entrance, staring at the end of
the wand as though transfixed.

Malvel twirled the wand slowly
through the air, making the scraps
of fur float. He spoke under his
breath:

"Beastly is as beastly does,
Change for me, and banish good."

Petra hadn't heard this spell before.
She watched as green smoke began
to billow around the dog. Whining,
the dog fell twisting onto its back.
All four legs kicked snow into the
air and the dog's spine arched as its
body writhed and contorted.

Petra backed away, her eyes
widening in horror.

"Excellent!" hissed Malvel. Even
he seemed surprised at how well his
spell was working.

The poor dog was panting now,
twitching and shuddering in the green
smoke. Petra gasped as she saw the
animal's thrashing body grow and
distort. Suddenly it turned over and
leapt to its feet. It towered over them.

Petra shrank back. There was no

sign of the miserable dog any more –
this Beast was a snarling evil monster.
His tongue lolled from his mouth,
spraying them with foul saliva, and his
eyes glowed with anger.

Petra stared at the huge paws, each
easily as large as her own head. The
Beast's fur glistened greasily and it
gave a loud growl.

Petra cowered down as the

monstrous dog leapt. But it sprang over her head and went loping away down the snowy mountainside, barking wildly.

"The spell worked. You've fulfilled your purpose, you mutt!" snarled Malvel. He lifted the wand again and pointing it towards the dog. Green smoke spurted through the air, chasing after the running Beast.

The smoke curled round the animal and with a dreadful howl it fell dead on the mountainside.

Petra stared at the wizard. "Why did you kill it?" she asked.

Malvel's lips curled in a slow smile. "I needed to be sure that my spell would work." He waved a dismissive hand at the fallen animal. "But it's clear now that I can create as many Beasts as I wish," he said. "And I have a very particular victim in mind!"

Petra frowned. "Who is this special victim?" she asked. "If I'm to help you, I need to know your plans."

Malvel glared at her. "Can you not guess?" he asked.

Petra looked anxiously up into the wizard's face. "Is it something to do with the poisoned meat you commanded me to leave in the back of the cave?" she asked.

"It is indeed," said Malvel. "I cast a binding spell over the meat – now we leave it here for the next victim."

"But who is the victim?" insisted Petra. "Another dog?"

Malvel stared at her. "No," he said. "Not a dog. Haven't you guessed yet? It's a wolf…" His eyes shone with malice. "Before this day is out, I'll have unleashed a Wild Terror!"

CHAPTER ONE

INTO THE FROZEN NORTH

Tom and Elenna smiled as the townsfolk gathered around Cora the shepherdess. Cora had been transformed by Petra the Witch into a terrible winged Beast named Koraka. But Tom had fought and defeated her, and the spell had been broken.

The friendly little boy, Fredo, ran

up to Tom and Elenna as they stood to one side with Tom's stallion, Storm, and Silver, Elenna's loyal wolf. He held out two bowls of hot stew.

"Thank you," Tom said, taking a bowl and spooning up the delicious food. "I'm hungry!"

"We both were," added Elenna.

Cris, Fredo's father, strode up, smiling broadly. "Will you stay to celebrate?" he asked. "You have done us great service and the least we can do is to hold a feast in your honour and give you warm beds for the night."

"We'd be grateful for any food you could give us, but we have to go," Tom said. His Quest was more important than any feast.

The man nodded, seeming to

understand. "I'll bring some food for the animals," he said, turning and striding away.

He returned with a bag of oats for Storm and a marrowbone for Silver to gnaw on. Tom and Elenna sat down to eat. Tom took out the parchment map that Petra had dropped when they'd first encountered her in Seraph.

Elenna leant close as he unfurled the tapestry map. In the past, it had always shown them their way forwards – and at the end of the path, an image of a new Beast would be displayed.

"There's where we must go," said Tom, tracing his finger along the thin silvery thread that wound from the town up through the hills and into the mountains of the north. "It looks like we're in for a cold journey."

"But there's no Beast shown at the end," said Elenna. "That's strange."

"Perhaps Malvel wants to spring a surprise," Tom suggested. "We should move quickly." Tom still ached from the bruising battle with Krakos, but his pains were well worth it if they were finally gaining the upper hand against Malvel and Petra.

After finishing the stew, they got up. Tom beckoned to Storm. The stallion clopped forwards with Silver the wolf trotting at his side.

Cris returned again with a bag of food for their journey. He looked over Tom's shoulder at the map. "I don't envy you that route," he said.

"We've been in cold places before," Elenna replied.

"It's not the cold that you need

fear," said Cris. "Packs of savage wolves roam those mountains."

He glanced at Silver, who stood at Elenna's side. "They aren't as loyal or obedient as your friend. The northern wolves are the only truly dangerous animals in all of Seraph. Be wary of them."

"We shall," said Tom. 'And thank you for the warning."

"I think I can do better than that," said Cris. "Wait a moment, and I'll find you some warm pelts." Cris vanished into a nearby hut and emerged a few moments later with his arms full of white fleeces.

Tom and Elenna pulled on thick waistcoats and tied them around their waists with leather thongs. There was even a large fleece to place under Storm's saddle.

Swaddled up in his fluffy white
coat, Tom struggled to pull his shield
up onto his shoulder.

"You look like an abominable
snowman!" Elenna laughed. But

it was Tom's turn to grin as she clambered awkwardly up onto Storm's back.

"And you look like a snowball with legs!" he teased, heaving himself clumsily up in front of her.

"I can give you a fleece to tie around your wolf, too," Cris said, carrying a final pelt.

Silver growled softly, and the fur stood up all along his spine. Cris backed away.

"I don't think he'll need any protection," Elenna said with a smile. "The cold won't worry him too much."

"So be it," said Cris, eyeing Silver uneasily. He raised a hand. "Farewell, and good luck!"

Tom flicked the reins and Storm broke into a brisk trot. The people cheered and waved as they rode out of the town, but Tom noticed a few looking nervously at Silver. He smiled – Elenna's pet could always be trusted.

As they made their way along a narrow road, Tom stared at the distant white mountains. It felt as though they were beckoning to him. Up there, somewhere, was the Eternal Flame. If Malvel managed to burn the Warlock's Staff in its fire, all kingdoms would be doomed, and their friend, Aduro, would be lost to them for ever. *We have no idea what type of Beast we'll meet up there*, Tom thought. *But that wasn't enough to stop him.*

"We only have three more Beasts to deal with," Elenna said over his shoulder, as though reading his thoughts. They had three tokens left, from the six created for them by Aduro – surely that meant three Beasts waiting for them.

"I know," Tom said, tightening his grip on Storm's reins. "I just hope the next one shows itself soon."

WHITE PERIL

They soon left the town far behind
as they made their way through the
beautiful landscape of Seraph. The sun
shone down from a clear blue sky and
deer grazed by bubbling streams.

"Seraph is so beautiful," sighed
Elenna. "It's hard to think of evil
in such a lovely place."

"I know," Tom agreed. "But Malvel
wants to destroy all that's here. That's

why we have to defeat him and return the Warlock's Staff to its rightful place." He set his jaw. "We have to save this kingdom."

"And Aduro?" Elenna asked.

It made Tom's chest hurt to remember how their friend, the good wizard of Avantia, had crumpled onto the floor, dead. "Him, too," Tom agreed. If they completed this Quest, there was a hope that Aduro could be brought back to life.

They rode on through groves and orchards, the ground beginning to rise. Ahead, distant white peaks lifted on the horizon. The snowy northern mountains shone brightly in the sunlight, but Tom remembered the warning Cris had given them.

Beware the wolves!

Elenna pointed over Tom's

shoulder. "Do you see that?"

A column of smoke spiralled up.

"I think it might be the Eternal Flame," said Tom.

"Do you think Malvel might already be there?" Elenna asked.

"I don't think so," Tom replied. "If Malvel had burned the Warlock's Staff, he'd already be spreading evil and misery."

Malvel had stolen the Warlock's Staff from the royal armoury in Avantia. By burning it in the Eternal Flame of Seraph, he would gain power over every known kingdom, and the Good Wizard Aduro would remain dead for all time.

I won't let that happen! Tom thought.

As they rode up into the hills, trees made way for thorny bushes. The streams ran cold and the hilltops were capped with snow. A chill wind blew down from the mountains.

Storm lowered his head, forging forwards against the cold, his hooves slipping on the ice. Soon, they were in a bleak, rugged world of snow and the companions began to breathe white mist.

Tom was glad of his bulky fleece – the icy air nipped at his ears and fingers. Only Silver seemed unconcerned as he padded along, leaving deep tracks in the snow, his tongue lolling, his eyes gleaming.

Suddenly Silver stopped, lifted his muzzle, and sniffed.

"What is it, Silver?" Elenna asked.

"I think he smells wolves!" said Tom, pointing ahead to where some dark shapes stood on the horizon. There were a dozen or more animals, with sharp ears and bristling coats.

For a few moments the wolves watched them. Silver gave a low, anxious growl, the fur rising along his spine.

Then the largest of the wolves turned slowly and loped away. A mournful howl shivered through the air. The other wolves turned and followed their leader, disappearing into the snow.

A few moments later the mountains echoed with a chorus

of howls. A cold dread crept down Tom's back at the eerie sound.

Storm was sweating and trembling with fear. Tom patted his neck. "They're gone," he murmured. "I won't let any harm come to you."

"Stay calm," Elenna told her wolf. The fur slowly flattened back down on Silver's back. Tom flicked Storm's reins and they continued their journey up the long slope towards the jagged-toothed mountain peaks.

The path narrowed between hulking shoulders of snow-covered rock. Once or twice, Storm's hooves slipped on patches of ice.

"I think we should dismount," Tom suggested. "It will be safer for Storm."

They climbed down and Tom walked ahead with Storm's reins held tightly in his fist. The rocks towered above them on either side, and the snow gathered in deep banks along their path. Tom tested each step before putting his weight down. Elenna and Silver kept close by.

The valley sides towered over them and the snow crunched underfoot as an icy wind blew into their faces.

"If we can just keep going..." Tom began.

There was a dreadful neighing from Storm. Tom felt the reins ripped from his hands. "Storm, what's wrong?" he cried, swivelling round.

Storm floundered in the deep snow that now came up to his knees. He was slipping backwards, backwards towards a crevice... Tom lunged for the flying reins, but before he could get a grip on them, the ground gave way under Storm's legs and the stallion fell, hooves kicking.

Tom flung himself forwards, managing to catch hold of the reins. But the weight of the falling horse dragged him headlong through the snow. Elenna leapt forwards, trying to grab his ankles.

Tom's eyes filled with ice and snow as he was pulled along on his stomach, clinging on grimly.

A great gulf had opened up under Storm, and as Tom blinked to clear his eyes, all he could see were kicking forelegs in a tumbling avalanche of snow.

"Quickly, Elenna! Help me!" Tom gasped. Elenna flung herself onto her front, snatching for the reins. But Tom's numbed fingers were no longer able to cling onto the leather straps, and before Elenna could catch hold

of them, they slid away as Storm
fell deeper into the chasm.

"No! Storm!" Tom shouted as he
saw the stallion's head vanish under
a billowing gush of snow.

Leaning out over the drop, Tom
wiped the snow from his eyes. There
was no sign of Storm. His horse had
been swallowed by the snow!

CHAPTER THREE

THE FROZEN CAVE

"Storm! Storm!"

Elenna caught hold of the thongs on Tom's fleece and held him back from falling over the edge. Silver was close by, barking and whimpering.

"Tom, I can't hold you if you lean out too far!" Elenna gasped.

A forlorn and desperate neighing rose up through the thick clouds of snow that billowed in the crevasse.

Storm was alive down there.

"Help me!" Tom said to Elenna. "We have to get down there. We have to dig him out. Look, there's a ledge!" He pointed towards a narrow shelf of ice jutting out from the crevasse wall.

Tom scrambled back until he was safe. Then he lowered himself over the edge of the chasm, stretching down until his feet found the ledge. He helped Elenna down and the two friends dropped carefully to their knees. There were more hand and footholds leading down into the crevice, and the occasional ledge; but it would be dangerous work climbing down.

"Are you with me?" Tom asked. "I can't leave Storm down there."

"Of course," she said.

Tom reached across to one of the shallow handholds that had been carved into the wall of ice by falling stones. The two of them slowly climbed down, until the sky was a narrow band of blue far above their heads. Silver followed, leaping from ledge to ledge.

Tom's limbs trembled with the

effort as he crept slowly down the rock face. His fingers slipped on the ice, and more than once he had to pause to catch his breath, clinging on with all his strength.

He heard Elenna give a cry as her feet skidded off a slippery ledge. She hung helplessly by her fingertips above him as Silver gave out an anxious howl.

"Don't move!" Tom called. "I'm right beneath you. Put your feet on my shoulders. I'll support you."

Elenna's feet rested heavily on his shoulders and he gritted his teeth as he strained to stay on the rock face. Taking a deep breath, he pushed upwards with all his might until her toes found the ledge again.

"Thank you!" she gasped. "I'm all right now."

Finally, they came to stand on soft piles of snow where Storm had fallen, in which he lay half buried. His eyes rolled back in his head and he gave a mournful neigh.

"Don't worry. We're here now," Tom told him.

They fell to their hands and knees and began to dig, heaving lumps of snow out of the way. Silver jumped down beside them and scrabbled frantically with his forepaws.

Tom's heart was in his mouth as they worked at the deep snow. Storm struggled fiercely to get free.

"His foreleg!" gasped Elenna. "Look! I think it's broken."

Tom bit his lip. Sure enough, Storm's left foreleg hung at an unnatural angle.

"Keep still, Storm!" Tom said.

"You'll only make it worse!"

The horse tossed his head but became quiet, almost as if he understood what Tom had said.

Tom cleared the snow from around the broken leg. His breath emerged in icy clouds, his fingers and toes growing numb in the cold. The thick fleece made his movements awkward and clumsy. Silver stood close by, belly-deep in the snow, watching them with worried eyes.

Tom took the green jewel he had won from Skor from his belt and pressed it gently to the wounded foreleg. The jewel glowed brightly and Storm neighed as the bones knitted and mended.

"You did it!" cried Elenna, throwing her arms around Storm's neck.

Tom gave a grim smile as he put

the jewel back into his belt. Elenna's
face was blue with cold and ice
crystals filled her hair.

"Now all we have to do is get out
again," he murmured.

Elenna stared up at the mouth of
the chasm. "How do we do that?"
she asked.

Tom looked around. The white
walls reared up on either side, ridged

with snow and covered with giant icicles. A cool, icy blue light filtered down from above. It was like being in a great open roofed palace of ice.

"Maybe we won't have to climb," he said. He pointed along a narrow path at the bottom of the crevasse. "We should go this way and hope for the best."

Tom, Elenna and Silver dug at the last of the snow until Storm was finally able to lurch free. The grateful horse nuzzled into Tom's neck.

"He's saying thank you," said Elenna.

"You're very welcome," Tom said, stroking the horse's head. He took Storm's reins and led him slowly along the deep winding floor of the crevasse.

At first, Storm limped on his

mended leg, as though nervous about putting his full weight on it. But soon he was walking normally.

It was deadly cold. Even the thick fleeces did not keep the chill from their bones, and Tom could feel drowsiness coming over him. His vision was blurring. He shook his head. He had to stay awake! If they fell asleep they would die.

Then Tom remembered the bell of Nanook that was embedded in his shield. It had the power to fight cold! He pulled the shield off his back and rubbed at the little silvery bell. Almost immediately, the whole shield began to glow and give out heat. For a few moments they all gathered around the shield, warming themselves before moving on.

Snow began to flurry into their

faces as they forged along the narrow valley. But Tom held the shield high, and the heat melted the snow in a wide arc ahead of them.

"I can feel my fingers again!" said Elenna.

As Tom pushed on, he became aware that the ground was rising under his feet. He looked up and saw that the towering walls were not so high as they had been. They were coming to the end of the crevasse. His instincts had been right!

They emerged out onto a high, snowy plateau. But they needed to find some shelter to recover.

"A cave!" Tom called, pointing ahead to a black hole in the mountainside.

They scrambled up the short path and gathered in the cave, glad of the chance to dry off. Storm and Silver moved deeper inside, as far from the icy air as possible.

Tom took the tapestry map out and examined it again. The path shown on the map led deeper into the mountains, but still there was no illustration of a Beast.

"Perhaps there won't be a Beast this time?" Elenna suggested.

Tom frowned. That had never happened before.

They heard a strange snuffling sound from the back of the cave, followed almost immediately by a loud whinny of distress.

"Storm?" Tom called, jumping up. "What's wrong?"

Elenna ran towards the two animals. "Silver?" she cried. "What's that you're eating?"

Tom ran after her. Silver was crouching at the back of the cave, his eyes glittering fiercely. He held a hunk of meat between his jaws and growled as Elenna stood over him.

"Let it go, Silver," Elenna said gently, reaching for the lump of

meat. "It may be rotten. It could make you ill."

Silver snarled, his lips curling to reveal his fangs as he slunk away from her. Tom stared at the wolf.

"Elenna?" he asked. "What's wrong with Silver?"

CHAPTER FOUR

ENCHANTED MEAT

Elenna caught hold of the meat that hung from the wolf's jaws. "Silver," she said sharply. "Let go!"

The wolf's eyes flashed with defiance, but he dropped the meat and moved deeper into the shadows at the back of the cave. Tom could hear his growls echoing off the walls.

Elenna moved into the light of the

cave mouth and examined the thick chunk of meat. There was something like green mould growing on it.

"It smells odd," she said, holding it up for Tom. He sniffed, his forehead wrinkling. "What's it doing here, anyway?"

Tom glanced into the cave. All that could be seen of Silver was a pair of glittering yellow eyes. "It must be rotten – it could have been lying here for months," Tom said.

Elenna shook her head. "It's not like him to eat bad meat," she said. "I can't think what came over him." She walked to the ledge outside the cave mouth and threw the meat far out into the snow.

"We should get moving," Tom said. He pointed towards a long sloping valley between rugged humps of rock.

"The map is leading us that way."

Elenna went into the cave. Tom watched as she found Silver sitting quietly in the darkness, his eyes wide and staring. "Are you all right?" she asked gently. "Has that bad meat upset your stomach?"

The wolf stood up, rubbing against her legs and allowing her to stroke his fur.

"Come on," she said. "We have to get going." She called to Tom. "I think he's fine after all!"

Obediently, the wolf trotted along beside her.

Tom was reluctant to mount Storm so soon after his injury, but the horse nudged against Tom's shoulder and neighed as if to prove he felt fine.

"Good boy!" said Tom as he and Elenna climbed onto Storm's back to continue their journey.

It was hard going, and bitterly cold, and although the snow had stopped falling, the clouds hung low and looked threatening. The orange glow of the Eternal Flame was ahead of them.

They plodded grimly through a narrow valley. The wind whistled, flattening Silver's fur along his back, gnawing at Tom's fingers and making

Elenna's teeth chatter.

Much more of this cold and even Nanook's bell won't keep us alive! Tom thought.

Storm kept his head down and his ears drawn back as he struggled onwards. The cold gripped Tom's head, making him feel faint and dizzy. Behind him, Elenna was swaying as though she could hardly stay on Storm's back. Even Silver was whimpering as he fought through the deep snow.

"There's a light!" cried Tom, pointing to a reddish glow in the snow ahead. "It looks like a fire."

"That means people," said Elenna. "Maybe even some hot food."

Tom nodded and tweaked the reins to guide Storm towards the glow. However important their Quest, Tom couldn't drive them to their deaths.

Coming over a rise, they saw a small encampment of tents around a large blazing wood fire. Sparks flew up as the logs crackled. Fur-clad people and shaggy dogs were gathered around the fire, and Tom could see a steaming cauldron hanging over the flames.

"They'll give us a good welcome, for sure," Tom said, urging Storm onwards. So far in their Quest, the people of Seraph had always been friendly and generous.

As they approached the camp, people stood up and watched them. Tom could see from their weathered faces and their thick animal-hide clothes that they were tough mountain-folk. One man stepped forwards and raised his closed fist.

Tom knew this gesture of greeting. He jumped down from the saddle and closed his own fist to press his knuckles against the man's.

"You pick cruel weather to travel here," said the man. He turned and gestured towards the fire. "Come, we have food to spare. Will you join us for a meal?"

"We will," Tom said. "Thank you."

The man noticed Silver. "You travel with a wolf?"

"He's good," Elenna explained. "There's no need for you to worry about him."

The man looked surprised. "I have never heard of such a thing!" he said. He walked back to the fire. "Come." He called to the people in the camp. "The strangers tell me there is nothing to fear. They say the wolf

57

has been tamed!"

Tom and Elenna followed him between the low tents, aware that the dogs and the people were watching Silver with unease.

"Give food to these weary travellers," said the man. "And fodder for the horse."

Elenna dismounted and they led Storm towards the dancing heat of the fire. As Silver came near the flames, he let out a low, menacing growl.

"Silver, there's nothing to be afraid of here," said Elenna. The wolf shot her a glance, his eyes reflecting the flames as though they leapt inside his skull. As Elenna moved towards him, he darted around the fire.

Tom gasped as a strange green smoke began to coil around Silver's legs. The dogs backed away, whining and howling. *Evil magic*, Tom thought. Before he could move, Elenna ran around the fire, calling anxiously: "Silver? Come to me, Silver."

His lips curled and he bared his teeth. Foam flecked his mouth and his eyes were wild with sudden fury.

Tom sprang forwards, pushing Elenna out of the way as the wolf leapt at her with snapping jaws.

"The wolf's not tame!" a voice howled. "Kill it! Kill it now!"

CHAPTER FIVE

DANGEROUS FRIEND

"No!" cried Elenna, running to protect Silver. "Don't kill him!"

"He's mad!" howled one of the people. "You can see it in his eyes!"

"Silver? What's wrong boy?" Elenna said in a soft voice.

Silver faced her, his head down, a terrible light in his eyes as he snarled and bristled.

"Something's happened to him,"
Tom shouted as some of the men
stepped forwards with daggers and
swords drawn. "This isn't like him.
Stand back – all of you!"

But one huge, bear-like man
pounced on Silver, taking him by
surprise. As the man drove him to
the ground, the wolf writhed,

twisting his head and snapping.

The man knelt down hard on Silver's chest, one hand gripping the long fur at the wolf's throat, the other arm raised, wielding a dagger.

Tom's hand was on his sword hilt.

"I'll cut the animal's throat!" the man shouted.

"No!" cried Elenna, hurling herself at him. Clamping her arms around his neck, she dragged him off Silver as the wolf howled and kicked.

Shouts of anger and warning came from the other people, but Elenna was on top of the man, seated astride his chest, her knees pinning his shoulders down. Before the man had the time to throw her off she pulled her bow from her back and fitted an arrow to the string.

"Keep still or I'll shoot," she

warned him, the point of her arrow aimed between his eyes. Her gaze flicked around the others. "And that goes for any of you. If you try to kill Silver, you'll pay for it, I promise you."

"She's as crazed as her wolf!" someone shouted. "Rush her! She can't shoot us all."

Tom sprang forwards. "Stand back!" he called. The people cried out angrily, their faces grim in the firelight.

Silver scrambled to his feet, the fur bristling like wire all along his spine, his eyes glittering with malice.

What's happened to Silver? This isn't right. Why has our loyal companion turned on Elenna like this?

With a long howl, Silver darted out of the firelight.

"It's running away!" someone shouted. "Stand back – let it go."

Silver raced off into the snow. Tom glanced at Elenna, seeing the misery and confusion on her face as their companion raced away from them.

Silver let out howls that made Tom's blood run cold. And there was something else; Silver was getting larger as he ran. He was changing before their eyes!

Tom snatched out the map and dropped to his knees, spreading it on the ground in front of him.

"No!" he moaned. The image of a Beast had finally appeared at the end of the silvery path. A huge and monstrous wolf! And below the image some intricate writing had formed.

"The Wild Terror," Tom muttered. Was that the name given to Malvel's newest Beast? Silver – the Wild Terror!

Tom got to his feet, his heart hammering wildly in his chest.

"Elenna," he called. "Put your bow away!"

Still glaring angrily at the sprawling man Elenna got to her feet and backed away. She looked along the line of pawprints that Silver had left in the snow. She released the tension in her bow and slid the arrow back into her quiver.

The man rose, picking up his fallen dagger. The other people were muttering angrily among themselves and those with weapons were moving towards Tom and Elenna.

"We have to go after Silver," Elenna

said, her face pale as she came to Tom's side. "He needs our help. He's ill."

Tom picked up the map and showed it to her. She gave a gasp of shock as she saw the image of the wolf. "No! Not Silver," she groaned.

"I think it is," Tom said, warily watching the approaching people. "And we've outstayed our welcome here. Stand back!" he shouted. "We're leaving."

"Yes! Go!" cried the man who had greeted them warmly only a short time ago. "You bring a savage animal here and then attack us when we try to defend ourselves from it. Are you out of your minds?"

"He's not savage!" Elenna cried. "There's something wrong with him."

"It's no good," Tom told her.

"They won't understand."

"We have to find Silver," said
Elenna. "We have to help him."

"Don't worry, we'll track him," Tom
told her. But he didn't dare say to
Elenna what he was thinking.

*If Silver's become a Beast, I may have to
fight him. Silver has been with us from
the start. He knows more about my
fighting skills than any other Beast.*

He spotted a sledge with a team of dogs still harnessed to it.

A sledge would cover the ground far more easily than Storm.

"We have to catch up with our wolf," Tom called to the grim-faced people. "Will you let us borrow a sledge?"

"Never!" shouted the first man. "And if you try to take it, we'll cut you down where you stand."

CHAPTER SIX

THE WOLF PACK

Tom hesitated, looking uneasily at the faces of the armed men. At least a dozen of them stood between him and the sledge. Normally, he avoided telling people about his Quests, but he had to convince these people to let him past.

"Listen to me, please," he called. "There's an evil wizard in Seraph called Malvel. He's powerful and will put your whole kingdom at risk if I can't defeat him. You must let us go." He gestured out over the snow. "Malvel's put an evil spell on our wolf – that's why he's out of control! I have to follow him and stop him."

Elenna came to his side. "It's true," she called. "Will you please help us?"

The face of the leading man grew less grim. The people of Seraph believed in being kind and generous to visitors – would he relent and help them?

"I have heard of monsters causing chaos in our realm," he admitted at last. "Perhaps they're the work of this Malvel?"

"They are," said Tom, meeting the man's gaze.

"Then we shan't delay you," he said. He turned to the others. "Let them leave. Be wary, but give them safe passage out of the camp."

Tom and Elenna exchanged relieved glances as the knives and swords were lowered.

"Come," said the man, beckoning as he strode towards the sledge. "I will give you the basic commands – the dogs will do the rest!"

Tom stepped onto the wooden sledge and unwound the long reins. Elenna climbed up behind and took a firm grip on the thongs binding Tom's fleece around his waist.

"Keep command of the dogs at all times," said the man. "To turn right, say 'gee', left is 'haw'. Say 'mush' to make the dogs run." He slapped Tom on the back. "Good luck!"

"Will you look after Storm till we return?" Tom asked. He had already

removed the pouch with the tokens
from Storm's saddle bag. Now, the
pouch was slung over his shoulder.

"We will tend to the animal," said
the man. "But if you do not return
the sled and our dog team by the full
moon, the horse is ours!"

"Agreed," said Tom.

The man stepped back and in
a loud voice shouted, "Mush!"

The team of dogs threw themselves
forwards, barking.

Tom and Elenna clung on tight as
the sledge glided along, slowly at
first, but getting faster. Tom glanced
over his shoulder to see the camp
falling away behind them.

The dogs ran on tirelessly, silently,
streaking through the deep snow,
heads down, tongues lolling.

Tom narrowed his eyes against the

rush of the cold wind, scanning the
horizon and hoping for some sign
of Silver. His fingers were already
numb. How long before his hands
became too chilled for him to grip
the reins?

They raced on over the snow,
speeding past pinnacles of glittering

frozen rock, shooting down long steep valleys where icicles hung like spears from high-ridged cliff faces.

At last, Tom spotted a small fleck of darkness moving across a field of snow to their right.

"Gee!" he shouted, his voice cracking from the cold air in his lungs. "Gee!"

The dogs responded, bringing the sledge around so that they were bearing down on the moving dot.

Gradually they closed in. Now Tom could see for certain that it was Silver. But the wolf had changed – he was bigger and more muscular, grown far beyond his normal size.

"Silver!" Elenna shouted. "Stop! We want to help you!"

"He won't understand you," gasped Tom.

But the wolf came to a halt at the sound of Elenna's voice. He turned and snarled at them.

Tom's heart missed a beat. Silver was almost unrecognizable. His face had become ugly and distorted, his eyes burned with a vicious light. His crooked, elongated jaws opened to reveal hideous slavering fangs. His claws had become long and curved like scythes, and his fur was thick and bristling, the hair along his spine stood up to form a row of sharp spikes.

Tom yanked back on the reins and the dogs came to a stumbling halt. They cowered in the snow, some of them whining as they stared at the great Beast that towered over them.

Tom and Elenna leapt off the sledge.

"What should we do?" Elenna cried. "I can't shoot at him! I can't!"

"We have to do whatever it takes to thwart Malvel's plans," Tom said grimly, resting his hand on the hilt of his sword. "Even if it means doing battle with Silver."

He took a step forwards, but the Beast lifted his great shaggy head and let out a loud, chilling howl.

Tom's ears were still ringing with the dreadful sound, when he saw what the Beast's howl had summoned. All along the horizon, dark shapes appeared. Wolves!

CHAPTER SEVEN

BELOVED ENEMY

The wolf pack moved forwards, watching the Beast for the command to attack. The sledge-dogs whimpered in fear as the Beast towered over them, his jaws dripping spittle.

"I'll get closer to him," Elenna said. "I may be able to calm him."

"He's in Malvel's thrall now," Tom warned her. "He may not even know who you are."

"I'm not going to give up on Silver," she said, slowly advancing. The huge Beast stared down at her, clouds of his icy breath billowing all around her as she approached. Tom thought he glimpsed a flicker of recognition in the Beast's eyes. *Did he remember her? Would she be able to soothe him?* he thought.

The wolves were slinking closer through the snow. How long did Elenna have before they attacked?

"Silver? It's me," she called to the Beast. "Your friend."

The Beast gave a shuddering howl and Elenna stumbled back, her bow in her hand.

The Beast leapt at her, his scythe-shaped claws reaching out. Elenna ducked sideways, fumbling for an arrow. But a claw sliced downwards,

tearing the quiver of arrows from
her back as she sprang aside.

"Get away from her!" Tom shouted,
lifting his shield high and throwing
himself forwards. Twisting his head
with terrible speed, the Beast clamped
the edge of Tom's shield between its
jaws and wrenched it away. With
a flick of its neck, the Beast sent it
skimming across the snow.

Tom unsheathed his sword in

one fast motion, slashing at the air with the blade, forcing the Beast to pull back. Tom caught Elenna's arm and dragged her away. He lunged forwards, sweeping his sword in a low arc. But the Beast seemed to anticipate the move, leaping high over the blade and springing forwards. Tom had to draw back as the jaws snapped a hair's breadth from his sword arm.

Scrambling away through the snow, Tom saw the Beast's evil eyes on them.

"He knows us too well," he gasped, his heart thundering. "He can anticipate everything we're likely to do."

"How can we defeat him?" Elenna asked.

Tom thought quickly. "By doing the unexpected," he said. "He's waiting for us to attack him, but let's split up

– circle him from either side and drive the other wolves off first."

The wolf pack crept closer, their yellow eyes bright and eager for prey, their fangs bared.

"Alright," Elenna said, nodding her head. "Let's do it."

Tom and Elenna sprang to either side of the Beast, racing over the snow. The Beast's huge head turned quickly from side to side. He hesitated, then flung out a clawed paw, first towards Tom, then towards Elenna. But he wasn't quick enough.

Elenna picked up her quiver of arrows and thrust it into her belt, quickly fitting an arrow to her bow and letting fly at the wolves. At the same moment, Tom flung himself towards his shield.

With a growl, the Beast turned on

Tom, rearing up on his hind legs, his claws extended, his fangs dripping green slime. Tom grabbed his shield and crouched behind it as the Beast leapt high into the air. The spikes along his spine clashed together, sending out a strange and eerie noise that made Tom wince.

The Beast crashed down with his full weight, fangs biting. But Tom touched his hand to his belt, drawing on the fighting skills of Tusk's amber jewel. He launched himself between the Beast's front legs.

The Beast howled in anger as Tom raced away under his body. But the Wild Terror spun around with incredible speed and launched himself high into the air, all four paws off the ground. *He means to crush me to death!*

Tom threw himself aside as the

Beast struck the snow. Tom got to his feet, but he was almost thrown down again as the ground rocked under him. Cracking, splintering sounds filled the icy air and fountains of freezing water spouted up.

There was the noise of swirling water. The weight of the Beast had smashed through the thick coating of snow-covered ice to uncover…

"It's a river!" Tom called to Elenna. Floes of ice bucked and rocked as the cracks spread. Great jets of water gushed up, splashing and foaming as the ice split and broke apart.

Tom only just managed to keep his balance on the rocking ice flow, as Elenna leapt to the riverbank.

Howling in anger, the Beast scrambled clear of the river – but he was now on the far side from Tom and Elenna and the other wolves.

Tom ran nimbly across the lurching ice floe and jumped to the snowy bank. But now the wolves had gathered around Elenna, howling and snapping at her.

"Get back!" Tom shouted, racing towards them with his sword.

Elenna was shooting arrow after

arrow. "Drive them into the river!" she called. "They'll be swept away."

Tom struck at the wolves with the flat of his blade and they howled with pain. Gradually he forced them down the steep bank of snow, swinging his blade again and again until his arms ached. Elenna loosed arrows that pierced the snow and ice beside the wolves' paws, forcing them to spring back. Now the wolves were backing away, snapping their jaws and howling with anger.

A few moments later and the first of the wolves went slithering down into the icy water. Tom and Elenna rushed forwards, driving the others on so that they fell over one another, whining as they slid into the river.

The creatures struggled and yelped as the freezing water swept them downstream, their fur plastered to their skinny bodies. At last they came to a place where the banks were lower and they were able to crawl out of the river. With bedraggled fur and their tails between their legs, they raced away, abandoning the Wild Terror.

The Beast let out a fearsome howl. For a moment, he stood glaring on the far side of the river, then he leapt. He came crashing down in the snow between Tom and Elenna, throwing them both off their feet.

Tom leapt up, remembering the pouch with the tokens in it. *That's it! I need to use a token.* Already three of the tokens had proved their value. Tom could only hope that one of them would help him defeat Silver, without harming him.

He pushed his hand into the pouch, which he'd hidden inside his tunic. His fingers closing around a phial. He drew it out and saw that it was made of thick glass with three brass rings around the neck, and a cork stopper. Inside was sparkling green powder.

It looks the same as the green dust on the meat that Silver ate! he thought. *But how do I use it against him now?*

A terrible growl sounded across the snow. Tom looked up and saw that the Beast had pounced on Elenna, ripping her bow and arrows from her hands and shoving her onto her back. As Tom watched in horror, the Beast's crushing jaws closed around Elenna's waist and lifted her high into the air.

CHAPTER EIGHT

RIDING THE WOLF

Tom launched himself at the Beast.

"Don't come near!" Elenna screamed, writhing as the Beast's jaws tightened around her. "Leave me! Get away."

"Never!" shouted Tom. "Not while there's blood in my veins!" As he leapt across the snow, he uncorked the phial of green powder.

The Beast kicked out fiercely. Tom

managed to lift his shield to block the blow. The deadly claws raked down the surface, and the impact sent him crashing onto his back in the deep snow.

He sprang up, somersaulting over the Beast's extended foot. His mouth and eyes filled with ice and snow and he could feel the coldness chilling his bones through his fleece as he rolled head over heels towards the Beast. *I'm nearly there…*

He sprang up under the Beast's towering flank. Gripping the phial, he flung his arm up, spraying a cloud of the powder over the Beast's fur.

Tom watched as the Beast lifted his huge head, shaking Elenna from side to side and filling the air with enraged growls. Elenna hung helplessly between the slavering

jaws – it was only the thick fur and the leather thongs of her fleece that were saving her flesh from being torn apart.

Nothing's happening! Tom thought desperately. *I chose the wrong token!*

Grimly, Tom clenched his fist around his sword; he had wasted a token, and now he would have to do battle with Silver.

But then he noticed that where a few flecks of the powder had fallen in the snow, thin wispy spirals of greenish smoke could be seen.

The Beast's fur was dry – but the snow was wet. Did the powder only work when mixed with water? He glanced into the phial – there were still a few grains of the powder left in the bottom. He dropped to his knees, to scoop snow into the bottle.

A vicious blow from the Beast's forepaw sent him tumbling across the ground. Another swipe grazed his cheek, drawing blood. Dizzy from the blow and grimacing in pain, Tom found himself sliding towards the icy river.

At the last moment, he managed to dig the rim of his shield into the snow to save himself from tumbling headlong into the rushing water. Gasping for breath, he realized that the Beast's attack had brought him to the perfect place for his plan.

He reached out a trembling arm and let the freezing water flow into the phial. Thick green smoke began to unfurl from the glass mouth. He heard the heavy thud of paws close by in the snow. Turning onto his back, he saw the Beast looming above him, Elenna still clenched in his jaws, one fearsome forepaw lifted, ready to tear Tom apart.

Tom thrust the phial up towards the Beast. The green smoke coiled and spread, writhing around the Beast's legs and climbing quickly up his body.

The Wild Terror's great eyes widened in dread as the smoke billowed around his head. Rearing up and trying to lift his muzzle above the smoke, the Beast's jaws slackened for a moment. Elenna didn't miss her chance. Twisting in the huge mouth, she pushed down hard on the lower jaw. With a snarl, the Beast released her. She tumbled down into the snow and lay there, silent and unmoving.

Tom had no time to go to her – he

had to finish the Beast off. If he didn't, Aduro would never be brought back to life, and Tom's Quest to defeat Malvel would fail.

He tucked the phial into this tunic then leapt to his feet. He flung himself at the Beast, snatching hold of the thick fur on his heaving flank and dragging himsclf upwards. The Wild Terror was howling in anger now, struggling to get free of the clinging green smoke. Tom coughed as he clambered up the Beast's body, the smoke filling his nostrils and lungs.

The Beast twisted his head, snapping at Tom with knife-sharp fangs and spraying him with spittle. Tom was high on the Beast's back, clinging to the hard spikes along his spine, refusing to be thrown off.

"Give it up," Tom cried. "Don't try to fight me!"

At last, Tom managed to straddle the Beast. But every muscle in his body was aching and the Beast was trying to throw him off. He only had a few moments before his strength gave out. Tom saw Elenna lying helpless in the snow. He took the phial out of his tunic. Green smoke was still seeping from the top. He pushed himself along the Beast's thrashing and twisting neck. *If I can just get to his eyes*, Tom thought.

He was almost there!

The Beast lifted his head, rose onto his hind legs and let loose a deafening howl. Tom had to cling to the fur with both hands to prevent himself from being flung to the ground. But as he snatched at the

bristling fur, the phial slipped from his fingers and went twirling away into the snow.

Tom felt his grip coming loose. He had failed. Malvel had beaten him at last.

CHAPTER NINE

THE WIZARD'S POWER

Clinging on desperately to the Beast's neck, Tom saw Elenna moving in the snow. She was waking up! Her head lifted and her eyes widened in fear as she saw the danger Tom was in.

"Get the phial!" Tom shouted. "Dip an arrow into the green liquid and shoot at the Beast!"

Elenna scrabbled through the snow

and snatched up the phial, rolling aside to avoid being trampled by the Beast's clawed paws. She was on her feet in an instant, drawing an arrow and dipping its tip into the bottle. She fitted the arrow to her bow and aimed the shaft at the Beast's head.

Tom saw tears brimming in her eyes as she stared up into the distorted face of the Beast that had once been her best friend.

"You can do it!" Tom cried down to her. "You have to! It's Silver's only chance of turning back to normal!"

"But if I miss, the arrow could hit you," Elenna called back.

"Don't worry about that!" Tom shouted down. "Shoot! Quickly!"

"I'm sorry, Silver!" Elenna said. Aiming between the Beast's eyes, she loosed the arrow. It sped straight and

true, striking the Beast's forehead
and sinking in deep.

The Beast gave a scream of agony,
rearing up on its back legs. Then it
shuddered and fell sideways, hitting
the snow with a great crash, sending
Tom sprawling.

"Silver!" Elenna cried. "Oh no! What have I done?"

The Beast lay unmoving in the snow, the arrow jutting from its head. Tom got to his feet, hardly daring to breathe. Was Silver dead?

But as the two friends approached the body of the Beast, Tom saw the arrow drop away. Elenna gave a cry of joy as the massive body began to shrink. The spikes along the spine fell apart and the hideous face and jaw shrank back until all that was left was the familiar face of their loyal wolf.

Silver stumbled to his feet, shaking his head as he fought to gain his balance.

"Silver!" Elenna cried. "I thought I'd killed you!"

Elenna's wolf padded unsteadily over to her. He opened his jaws

and licked her hand.

Elenna flung her arms around
Silver's neck and buried her face in
his fur.

A furious voice rang out. "So, you
have defeated another of my Beasts!"

Tom spun around in alarm. Malvel
was standing behind him, his eyes
blazing in anger, his wand pointed at
Tom's heart. A horrible stench came
from the wand and Tom stared in
disgust at the teeth embedded in it
and the strips of fur-covered leather

that swung from the handle.

"You will not defeat me again!" roared the wizard. A jet of green smoke burst from the end of the wand and snaked rapidly towards Tom. He was quick enough to throw his shield up to deflect the worst of it, but green tendrils of smoke crept around his shield, catching in his throat and filling his nostrils with a vile stink. He leapt sideways as the foul green smoke pursued him.

"Haven't you done enough harm, Malvel?" Tom shouted. "Leave this realm in peace."

"Never," howled the wizard. "I came to Seraph to win ultimate power, and I will not leave until I get it."

The sky above their heads suddenly erupted in a burst of fire. Tom fell

back with a gasp. It was the Eternal
Flame of Seraph, burning fiercely on
the mountaintop and throwing a
bright orange glow over the snow
and ice.

Malvel stared at the blazing flame
with glowing, triumphant eyes. He
ran across the snow and leapt onto
Tom's sledge. "Run, you miserable
wretches!" he howled at the dogs.
"On your feet! I command it! Take
me to the Eternal Flame!"

The dogs sprang up and began to
drag the sledge towards the mountain
where the flame flickered.

Tom started to run, but the sledge was
moving too fast. He would never catch
up with it. Then he heard the thud of
hooves in the snow behind him.

"Tom, watch out!" Elenna shouted.
"It's Petra!"

Tom sprang aside as the witch's black unicorn went thundering past with Petra on its back. She'd had this unicorn since Tom had first encountered her in Seraph, its good nature had been twisted to evil.

"Malvel!" Petra called in a thin, plaintive whine. "Wait! Don't leave me behind."

Tom watched as the unicorn gathered speed and rose into the air. Petra had almost caught up with the racing sledge. Another moment and she would be able to leap on board.

But even as she reached out, Malvel turned and lashed at her with his whip. With a startled cry, Petra tumbled headlong from the flying unicorn and came crashing down into the snow.

"No!" She staggered to her feet,

calling out in desperation as the
sledge sped away over the horizon
with her black unicorn flying behind.
She dropped to her knees with a
wailing cry.

Tom shook his head, grimly. Malvel
hadn't just stranded Tom and
Elenna – he'd abandoned the little
witch!

CHAPTER TEN

AN UNEASY ALLIANCE

Tom and Elenna pounded through the snow to where the witch was kneeling. Silver streaked ahead, snarling and bristling.

"No, Silver!" Tom called as the wolf closed in on Petra. "Don't hurt her." Silver pounced at Petra and closed his jaws on her cloak to prevent her from escaping.

Petra's head was bowed and they could hear her moaning softly to herself. The tracks of the sledge stretched away over the horizon. Malvel was gone.

Elenna reached out a hand, but Petra brushed it aside. Clumsily, she got to her feet, Silver's teeth still clamped on the end of her cloak. She turned, her eyes hard.

"Get away from me or I'll strike you down," she snarled.

Tom gazed into her petulant face. "Is that wise, now that your master has left you behind?" he asked.

"Let her go, Silver," said Elenna. The wolf opened his jaws and Petra glowered at him as she gathered her cloak around her.

"Malvel was never my master," she snapped. "He only thought he was."

"You're hurt," said Elenna, seeing cuts and grazes on the witch's hands and face. "Let me help."

"I don't need your help," Petra spat, her eyes blazing. Then her expression softened and a cunning look came into her eyes. "Do you think Malvel left me behind?" She gave a shrill cackle that set Tom's teeth on edge. "That was all part of my plan." She gave a crooked grin. "Malvel will never reach the Eternal Flame." Her eyes flickered from Tom to Elenna. "But with my help, I'm certain that the two of you will.'

Tom stared at her in disbelief. "You want to help us?" he gasped.

Petra drew herself up and gave him a haughty look. "If you're clever enough to become my allies, I will help you," she said. "I expect you'd

be interested in knowing some of
Malvel's deepest secrets?"

"We would," agreed Elenna. "But
we'd never trust you to tell them
to us."

Petra's lip curled. "And I thought
we would become such great
friends," she said. "You disappoint
me. I may have to seek the Eternal
Flame without you, then." She

turned as if to walk away. Silver growled at her, his eyes glinting. "Good wolfie," she muttered, uneasily.

Tom bit his lip to stop himself from laughing. It didn't look as though she was going very far.

"No hard feelings, I hope?" she said. "I was only joking about leaving. I wanted Malvel to leave me here with you. That's how I'd always planned it."

Tom knew when he was being lied to. "He left you face down in the snow. You were desperate not to be left behind," he said.

The smile fell from the little witch's face. "I promise I'll tell you his secrets," wailed Petra. "Take me with you."

"Take you where?" asked Tom. "We're in the middle of this frozen wasteland with no sledge or horse."

"I wouldn't be so sure of that," said Elenna, pointing away behind Tom. "Look!"

He turned. A small dark shape was moving rapidly over the snow, following the sledge tracks up from the lower slopes of the mountains.

The shape grew large enough for Tom to recognize it. "Storm!" he called. "He must have sensed that we'd need him."

The great black stallion neighed as he came running towards them. Silver barked, glad to see his friend again.

Snorting and shaking his mane, Storm nuzzled into Tom's shoulder.

"Good boy!" Tom said, patting his neck.

Elenna turned to where the glow

of the Eternal Flame threw down its orange light. "We should get moving," she said. "Malvel has quite a lead on us."

"What about me?" whined Petra.

"I don't trust you," Tom said slowly. He looked into her sly face. Despite himself, he couldn't ignore the twinge of guilt that pulled at his heart. *I can't just abandon her to die here*, he thought. Perhaps if he kept her with him, she would prove useful. "You can come along with us," he said at last. "Elenna, get some rope out of the saddlebag. We're going to bind her hands."

Petra's forehead wrinkled. "But how am I to ride with my hands tied?" she asked.

"You're not going to ride," Tom told her. "We're going to ride. You're going to walk."

Elenna wound a length of rope around Petra's wrists and secured it with tight knots. Then the two of them climbed onto Storm's back, as the little witch glowered up at them.

"And you'd better start telling us some of Malvel's secrets," Tom said as Storm began to trot through the snow, pulling Petra along with him. "We still have two Beasts to defeat if we are to fulfill this Quest."

The four companions headed deeper into the snowy mountains, Silver growling menacingly as he followed at Petra's heels.

Tom looked down at the little witch. Would she be a help or a hindrance? She was the most unlikely ally they'd ever had. He couldn't help but wonder what

challenges lay ahead. An orange light glowed in the far distance. Two more Beasts to conquer, and then they'd arrive beside the Eternal Flame.

We're nearly there, Tom thought. But there was still a lot to survive yet. He just hoped that Petra wouldn't get in the way of his Quest.

Join Tom on the next stage
of the Beast Quest when he meets

SPIKEFIN
THE WATER KING

Win an exclusive
Beast Quest T-shirt and goody bag!

Tom has battled many fearsome Beasts and we want to know
which one is your favourite! Send us a drawing or painting of
your favourite Beast and tell us in 30 words why you think
it's the best.

Each month we will select **three** winners to receive
a Beast Quest T-shirt and goody bag!

Send your entry on a postcard to
BEAST QUEST COMPETITION
Orchard Books, 338 Euston Road, London NW1 3BH.

Australian readers should email:
childrens.books@hachette.com.au

New Zealand readers should write to:
Beast Quest Competition, PO Box 3255, Shortland St,
Auckland 1140, NZ or email: childrensbooks@hachette.co.nz

**Don't forget to include your name and address.
Only one entry per child.**

Good luck!

Join the Quest,
Join the Tribe

www.beastquest.co.uk

Have you checked out the Beast Quest website? It's the place to go for games, downloads, activities, sneak previews and lots of fun!

You can read all about your favourite beasts, download free screensavers and desktop wallpapers for your computer, and even challenge your friends to a Beast Tournament.

Sign up to the newsletter at www.beastquest.co.uk to receive exclusive extra content and the opportunity to enter special members-only competitions. We'll send you up-to-date info on all the Beast Quest books, including the next exciting series which features six brand-new Beasts!

All books priced at £4.99,
special bumper editions
priced at £5.99.

Orchard Books are available from all good bookshops, or can
be ordered from our website: www.orchardbooks.co.uk,
or telephone 01235 827702, or fax 01235 8227703.

Series 9: THE WARLOCK'S STAFF
COLLECT THEM ALL!

Malvel is up to his evil tricks again! The fate of
all the lands is in Tom's hands...

URSUS
THE CLAWED ROAR

978 1 40831 316 9

MINOS
THE DEMON BULL

978 1 40831 317 6

KORAKA
THE WINGED ASSASSIN

978 1 40831 318 3

SILVER
THE WILD TERROR

978 1 40831 319 0

SPIKEFIN
THE WATER KING

978 1 40831 320 6

TORPIX
THE TWISTING SERPENT

978 1 40831 321 3

Series 10: Master of the Beasts
Out March 2012

Meet six terrifying new Beasts!

Noctila the Death Owl
Shamani the Raging Flame
Lustor the Acid Dart
Voltrex the Two-Headed Octopus
Tecton the Armour-Plated Giant
Doomskull the King of Fear

978 1 40831 517 0

Watch out for the next Special Bumper Edition Grashkor the Death Guard! OUT JAN 2012!

SPECIAL BUMPER EDITION!

FROM THE DARK, A HERO ARISES...

Dare to enter the kingdom of Avantia.

A new evil arises in Avantia. Lord Derthsin has ordered his armies into the four corners of Avantia. If the four Beasts of Avantia can find their Chosen Riders they might have the strength to challenge Derthsin. But if they fail, the land of Avantia will be lost forever…

FIRST HERO, CHASING EVIL, CALL TO WAR, FIRE AND FURY OUT NOW!

www.chroniclesofavantia.com